BENNY SHARK

Goes to Friend School

by LYNN ROWE REED

Illustrated by RHODE MONTIJO

two lions

To Finnegan Ice
—L. R. R.

For all the little fish out there—
never give up!
—R. M.

Published by Two Lions, New York

www.apub.com

Amazon, the Amazon logo, and Two Lions are trademarks of Amazon.com, Inc., or
its affiliates.

ISBN-13: 9781477828038 (hardcover)
ISBN-10: 1477828036 (hardcover)

The illustrations are rendered in watercolor with pen and ink and digital coloring.
Book design by AndWorld Design

Printed in China
First Edition

10 9 8 7 6 5 4 3 2 1

BENNY SHARK was big, bad, and bossy.
Worst of all, he was a BULLY!

Benny loved making the other
sea creatures tremble and shake.

At lunch he growled to Cranston Crab,
"GIMME YOUR GRUB, OR I'LL CRUSH YOUR CRUSTY CLAWS!"

. . . and no one to play with.

Sometimes Benny was left out of the fun.

So Benny decided to get some friends.

"*BE MY FRIEND!*" he barked to Janice Jellyfish.

"It doesn't work that way," Janice answered. "To have a friend, you must first *be* a friend. You can learn at Friend School."

Really? Even a bull shark like me?

YES!

And off they swam to school.

"Welcome to Friend School!" said the teacher, Ollie Octopus.
"He means the friendless school!" Benny snickered and nudged
Larry Lobster.
But Larry ignored him.

"There are many rules for being a friend," Ollie said. "Let's get into groups and practice Rule Number One."

RULE #1: A FRIEND IS A GOOD LISTENER.

Benny looked around, but he had no one to talk to. So he butted in. "What are you shrimp talking about?"

"Benny, listen first," said Ollie.

So Benny listened.

But Benny did not say that to the shrimp.

"I'm glad you're trying, Benny," said Ollie, "but that's not *exactly* what I meant. Friends should also be polite."

"Sorry," Benny said to Janice.

"I forgive you," Janice said.

RULE #3: A FRIEND SHARES.

Benny had even more rules to learn.

At lunch Benny shared his food with his new friends.

Ten for me and one half for each of you.

At recess Benny practiced the next rule. Janice wanted to dress up in tutus, but Benny wanted them to play Marco Polo. Benny said, "Let's play Marco Polo first. We'll play tutus later. I *promise*."

But recess ended before tutu time.

RULE #5: A FRIEND IS A GOOD SPORT.

Ollie said, "Students, I think you'll like the next rule! To practice it, we will race! Benny and Janice will go first."

Benny loved racing because he was *fast*. Benny LOVED to win!

"Let's wear tutus to race," Janice said to Benny.

"No thanks," Benny said. "But if you beat me, I'll wear the tutu. I *promise*."

Benny and Janice lined up.
"On your mark . . . get set . . . *SWIM!*"
shouted Ollie Octopus.

Benny got off to a fast start.
But Janice swam faster . . . and faster . . .

. . . until she passed Benny.

Soon Janice ran into trouble.

Benny saw his chance to get ahead. He swam even faster.

That'll slow her down.

But then Benny heard Janice cry out.

HELP ME, BENNY!

No one had ever asked for Benny's help before.

He thought about how Janice had invited him to Friend School and how she forgave him when he was mean.

Janice is a true friend!

This was his chance to win . . .

Benny and Janice crossed the finish line together.

And even though Benny didn't win the race, he was happy that his friend was safe.

The next day, Benny Shark was ready to graduate with his friends. They all wore caps and gowns except for Benny, who practiced one last rule . . .